FOR
SALE
MOVING!

TO
CONNOR

Bruce's BIG MOVE

RYAN T. HIGGINS

Disney · HYPERION

Los Angeles   New York

For Rotem

This book is set in Macarons/Fontspring
Designed by Phil Caminiti
Illustrations were created using scans of treated clayboard for
textures, graphite, ink, and Photoshop

Library of Congress Cataloging-in-Publication Data

Names: Higgins, Ryan T., author, illustrator.
Title: Bruce's big move / by Ryan T. Higgins.
Description: First edition. · Los Angeles ; New York : Disney-Hyperion, 2017.
Sequel to: Hotel Bruce. Summary: "With four geese, three mice, and a
very grumpy bear all crowded into one den, Bruce is ready for a new
home"—Provided by publisher.
Identifiers: LCCN 2016054230 · ISBN 9781368003544 (hardback)
ISBN 1368003540 (hardcover)
Subjects: CYAC: Bears—Fiction. Animals—Fiction. Moving.
Household—Fiction. Humorous stories. BISAC: JUVENILE FICTION /
Animals / Bears. JUVENILE FICTION / Family / Alternative Family.
JUVENILE FICTION / Humorous Stories.
Classification: LCC PZ7.H534962 Bru 2017 DDC [E]—dc23
LC record available at https://lccn.loc.gov/2016054230

Reinforced binding

Visit www.DisneyBooks.com

Publisher's Note: The recipe contained in this book is to be followed exactly as written, under adult supervision.
The Publisher is not responsible for your specific health or allergy needs that may require medical supervision.
The Publisher is not responsible for any adverse reactions to the recipe contained in this book.

Bruce was a bear who lived with four geese because he was their mother,

and three mice
because they would not leave.

and make a big mess.

Bruce's house was crowded, chaotic, and loud.

CANNONBALL!

And he didn't like it one bit.

Bruce wished there was a way to get rid of the pesky rodents.

But there wasn't.

He DID try.

And try . . .

. . . and try.

So Bruce decided to move.

Finding a new house for a mother bear and his four geese can be difficult.

But Bruce found the perfect new house eventually.
It was in a quiet neighborhood,
with a lake, meadows nearby to explore . . .

... and plenty of friendly neighbors for the geese to play with.

I'm Hilda! And these are my 13 sisters. We're going to be best friends!

Bruce did not like friendly neighbors.

The best thing about the new house
was that there were no mice.

So Bruce was happy.

But the geese
were not.

Bruce tried cheering them up....

Nothing worked.

Until the moving van arrived.

Now the geese were happy.

And the mice were happy.

Bruce was not.

Bruce's house was once again crowded, chaotic, and loud.

And Bruce didn't like it one bit.

But it felt like home.

Grammie Tootie's Applesauce
- 8 apples
- 1 cup of water
- 1 tsp. of cinnamon
- 1/2 cup brown sugar

Peel, core, and chunk apples. Put
ingredients into Crock-Pot. Cover and
cook on high for 2 to 3 hours. Check
and mash apples every 20 minutes.
Once applesauce has reached right
consistency, continue cooking on high
for 2 to 3 additional hours.
SERVE HOT!

FOR BRUCE
FROM
NIBBS